To Esme, Happy Christmas love from Philip & Alex

D0188198

This book is dedicated
to my family.

a templar book

First published in the UK in 2010 by Templar Publishing,
an imprint of The Templar Company Limited,
The Granary, North Street, Dorking, Surrey,
RH4 1DN, UK

www.templarco.co.uk

Copyright © 2010 by Owen Davey

First edition

ISBN 978-1-84877-125-3

Printed in China

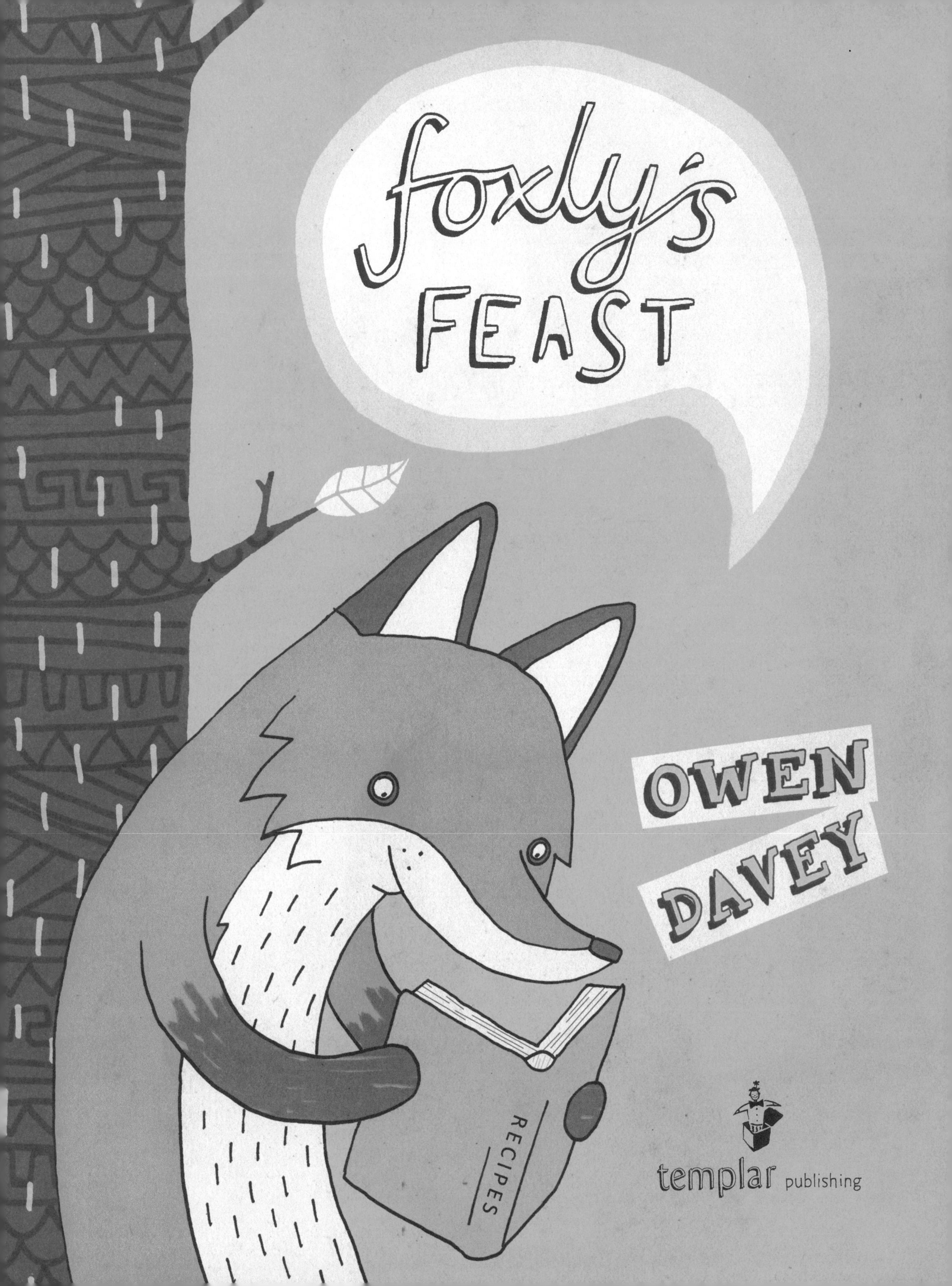

foxly's FEAST

OWEN DAVEY

templar publishing